Stin

Megan McDonald

Superhero Superfan

illustrated by

Peter H. Reynolds

CANDLEWICK PRESS

Text copyright © 2023 by Megan McDonald
Illustrations copyright © 2023 by Peter H. Reynolds
Stink® is a registered trademark of Candlewick Press, Inc.

First edition 2023

Library of Congress Catalog Card Number 2021946668
ISBN 978-1-5362-1507-6

22 23 24 25 26 27 LBM 10 9 8 7 6 5 4 3 2 1

Printed in Melrose Park, IL, USA

This book was typeset in Stone Informal and hand-lettered by the illustrator.
The illustrations were created digitally.

Candlewick Press
99 Dover Street
Somerville, Massachusetts 02144

www.candlewick.com

For my friends at Walker Books Australia
MM

To Don Rosa, comic book legend,
and Marzia Caramazza, comic superfan!
PHR

CONTENTS

Superheroes on the Brain 1

Too Grool for School 17

Super Gecko Yard Sale 35

Pinkie, Pinkie Cowbell 51

Whodunit? 67

Doctor Octopus 87

Ninety-Nine Cents 103

Superhero Science 119

Geckoheads forever 133

aboom!

    Ka-tang!

    Ka-pow!

Stink Moody was a real-life crime fighter. For a day, that is. Stink and Riley Rottenberger were at Saturday Science Club. They were learning about forensic science from Mrs. Rottenberger, their teacher and Riley's mother.

Stink got to use a pocket microscope. Stink got to track footprints. Stink got to dust for fingerprints. Stink and Riley spent all morning finding clues, adding them up, and solving a mystery.

"We're out of time for today," said Mrs. Rottenberger.

"Too bad," said Riley. "I love puzzles and mysteries."

"Forensic science is cool," said Stink. "I liked when we got to spot the difference between photos. And when we compared handwriting in those notes."

"Next Saturday, everybody, we're going to explore superhero science,"

said Mrs. Rottenberger. "Could the Flash really run across water? Could *my* favorite superhero, Elastigirl, aka Mrs. Incredible, stretch herself to be as tall as the Statue of Liberty? We'll have water-drop races and make superhero slime to find out."

Stink couldn't believe his not-super-sonic ears! Stink was cuckoo for super-heroes. "Superhero science!" said Stink. "*Shazam!* That sounds even better than crime-fighting science!"

"Thanks," said Riley. "It was my idea."

Stink imagined himself in a cape that said STINK: SUPERHERO SUPERFAN.

"What superhero powers you would

like to know more about?" asked Mrs. Rottenberger. "X-ray vision? Invisibility? Speed? For next Saturday, choose one superpower that you'd like to explore, and we'll find out the science behind it."

All the way home, Stink thought about superheroes and their superpowers. Wonder Woman flew on air currents. Maybe they could measure wind speed. Cool! Superman had X-ray vision.

Spider-Man had his spidey sense. And he could shoot webs from his fingers. Black Panther's suit could make him invisible, and he could see in the dark. The Flash was super speedy and traveled through time.

Wait! What about Green Lantern's power ring? Could science explain how it created a force field around him?

When Stink got home, his whole family was cleaning out the garage.

Dad was dusting off old records. Mom was painting an old chair. Judy was making a sign with squeaky markers.

Stink used his super powers of observation and deduction. This could mean . . . They were moving? Getting a new car? Having a yard sale?

Judy held up her sign. "Check it out, Stink." YARD SALE! COOL STUFF!

"Yard sale! *BAM!* I knew it!" said Stink. "Can I sell stuff, too?"

"Maybe you can sell some of the action figures and toys that you don't play with

anymore, Stink," Mom said.

"Okay, but not my Batmobile or Green Lantern power ring," said Stink. "Hey! Maybe I can make enough to get a Black Panther vibranium power-claw bank."

"A whosie whatsit?" asked Judy. "Stink, you have superheroes on the brain."

"Yeah, I do!" said Stink. "Because I have to come up with a superhero power to explore next week at Saturday Science Club."

"Pick Squirrel Girl! She has a rhyming name like me," said Judy. "Doreen Green. And she has the superpowers of a squirrel. She can jump between trees and chew

through wood with her teeth. Or pick the Flash. He can speed-read."

"How about Black Panther?" said Stink. "He can see in the dark. Or what about Spider-Man's spidey sense? He senses danger from miles away."

"I can sense that you're in danger of not making any money if you don't get a move on," said Mom.

Stink ran upstairs lightning-bolt-fast like the Flash. He filled up a laundry basket with stuff he could sell—old tub toys, toe socks, a piggy bank (really a hippo bank), and a genius kit that had not made him a genius.

"Look at all this stuff I can sell," said Stink. "I'm going to be rolling in it!"

"You're selling your piggy bank?" Judy asked. "But you love saving money."

"This is just my one-eared *hippo* piggy bank," Stink told her. "I still have my gumball-machine piggy bank. But if I sell this one, I can make tons of money and get the Black Panther vibranium power-claw bank. It has flashing lights and sounds and an actual claw reaches out to take your money! It holds six hundred coins, one hundred dollar bills, *and* it's password protected," said Stink.

"Is the password going to be *power claw*?" Judy asked.

GULP! "No," he said, staring at the ground. "Well, maybe. Okay, yes, but—"

"Stink, maybe you should hang on to that genius kit," said Judy.

The next day, Grandma Lou came to help with the yard sale. She brought a few things of her own to sell: a cowboy lamp, Christmas candlesticks, and an old canary cage.

"Yard sale time!" said Grandma Lou. "I like the chalk footprints leading people up the sidewalk to your house."

"Thanks," said Stink. "That was my idea."

"Did you put up some signs, too? Signs are important."

"I made signs using smelly markers," said Judy. "I put them up on telephone poles at both corners of our street."

"Sweet *and* stinky," said Stink, "so people can smell their way here."

"Good. I hope we get some buyers, not just lookie-loos," said Grandma Lou.

"What are lookie-loos?" Stink asked.

"You know, people who come just to look, but don't buy anything."

"For sure someone's going to want my bouncy ball collection," said Judy. "And this potholder loom. And my old cash register."

"Cash register?" asked Stink. "Can I have that?"

"Sure," said Judy. "That'll be one dollar."

"Sold," said Stink.

"Where's my dollar, Stink?" Judy asked.

"Um, I don't have it yet. But I will. I'm going to sell my old yo-yos with missing strings. These are gonna sell like cupcakes."

"You mean hotcakes," said Judy.

Stink shrugged. "Then I can pay you back and have enough for my power-claw bank."

"Never mind. Just pay me two gum-wrapper chains, one wind-up birthday cake, and one mini-eraser." She took them out of Stink's laundry basket.

Stink eyeballed some shelves in the garage. "Hey, has anybody come across a shoebox filled with my origami creations? I think I could sell those, too!"

Nobody answered. They were already talking to early-bird customers.

Stink stood on a stepladder and pulled down an old shoebox covered in thick dust. But the shoebox was not filled with origami. It was filled with old comic books! *Super Gecko: Tales to Amaze and Astonish. Super Gecko: Part Lizard, Part Man, All Superhero. Super Gecko Gets in a Sticky-Wicky Situation.*

On every cover was a freaky green lizard man. Beside him was a burst that read *HELLO, FUN! He defies gravity! He sees colors in the dark! He catches enemies with the flick of a tongue! He has the sticking power of an intermolecular force!*

Stink came down off the ladder and started reading. *Flip, flip, flip.* He could not stop turning pages.

"Stink," said Judy, but Stink wasn't listening.

Stink had never heard of a gecko superhero before! *Cheek! Chack! Chirp!*

"Stink, your friends are—"

This gecko was super sleek like Black Panther. This gecko was super speedy, faster than the Flash. This gecko could climb walls better than Spider-Man. He was funny, too. He said stuff like "Spooky spaghetti!" and "What a sticky-wicky situation!"

Stink ran to show his family. "This superhero can climb walls, scale buildings, and hang from ceilings. He can stick to anything!"

"Is that . . . Super Gecko?" asked Dad, squinting. "Hello, fun!"

Grandma Lou came over. "These were mine when I was a girl," she told Stink, "and I passed them on to your dad when he was your age."

"He's green. He's unseen. He's a climbing machine," said Dad.

"Super Gecko to the rescue!" said Grandma Lou, raising one arm in the air.

"Can I see?" asked Sophie of the Elves.

"Can I see?" asked Webster.

"Hey, where did you guys come from?" Stink grinned at his friends.

"I've been trying to tell you, gecko brain," said Judy. "Your friends are here." She went back to her table to sell stuff.

"We came to check out the yard sale," said Sophie. "I'm looking for unicorns."

"I'm looking for action figures," said Webster. "Got any *luchadores*?"

"I might," said Stink. "But first, you gotta see this. Super Gecko is so fly. He was just this teenage surfer dude in Hawaii, right? Then there was a volcano under the sea and he got hit by a supersonic tsunami. When he woke up on the beach, his wet suit had turned emerald green. And he had scales and a tail. And superpowers like a gecko!"

All three of them pored over the comic books.

"I can't believe you saved those old comics all these years," Grandma Lou said to Dad.

"Are you kidding?" Mom teased. "I had one dilly of a pickle just to get him to box them up and move them to the garage."

"Ha, ha, very funny," said Dad.

"I just sold my string collection!" said Judy. "And a scratched-up Magic 8 Ball and my potholder loom and a bag of potholder loops." Nobody paid attention.

"Check this out!" said Sophie. "Super Gecko has a sidekick, Gecko Girl!"

"Gecko Girl helps Super Gecko trick the evil Teflon Man," said Webster.

"Super Gecko can stick to anything," said Dad, "anything but Teflon."

"He sticks better than Super Glue!" said Stink.

"And he's left-handed," Dad told Stink.

"Like me and you!" said Stink. "*Shazam!* A left-handed superhero."

"He wasn't always left-handed," said Dad. "But in one of the adventures, he loses his left arm and it grows back much stronger than his right arm ever was."

"Super Gecko is cool," said Stink.

"He's not just cool," said Dad. "He's GROOL. Look on the back cover."

Stink turned the comic book over. "Super Gecko is great. Super Gecko is cool. Great plus cool equals GROOL!"

"Too grool for school!" shouted Webster and Sophie.

How to draw Super Gecko

1.

2.

3.

4. BODY LINE

5. 2nd BODY LINE

6. RIGHT ARM • LEFT ARM BIGGER

7. PANTS • LEGS • Feet

FOUR "TOES"
Real Geckos have five.

8. CAPE • SCALES • STRIPES ON PANTS

then... ADD COLOR!

Judy waved Stink over to one of the tables. "Stink! You have a customer!"

His customer was a teenager with pink hair. She had holes in her jeans and a spiderweb painted on her face.

"If you're looking for face paints, I don't have any," Stink told her. "Or patches for pants. How about a yo-yo without a string?"

The girl laughed. "I'm not here for that. I heard you guys talking and I want to buy your Super Gecko comics." Out of her back pocket she pulled a double sawbuck. A real live twenty-dollar bill!

Stink's eyes got big. Stink's eyes got round. He looked over at Dad and Grandma Lou. "Um. They're not really mine to sell," he told her.

"It's OK," said Dad. "You can sell them or keep them: your choice."

Twenty whole dollars! That was a lot of loot. But . . .

"I don't know," said Stink. "I just found them. I haven't even read them all yet."

"I'll be over by the records while you think about it," said Pink Hair Girl.

"What if they're worth a lot of money?" said Webster.

"Like ten dollars *each*," said Sophie.

"Or twenty. Or fifty. Or one hundred," said another familiar voice. "Super Gecko comics are way old."

Riley Rottenberger!

"Hi, Stink," said Riley. She held up a soda-can robot with googly eyes. "Does this robot actually do anything?"

"Wait," said Stink. "You know about Super Gecko?"

Riley nodded. "My uncle collects old comic books. If you have a rare one, it can be worth a ton of money. Like a thousand dollars."

"For real?" asked Stink.

"Sure. Like the Phantom. He came
before Superman and Batman. And
Doc Savage. He used brain power to
fight crime without a cape."

"Geez," said Stink. He turned a page
of the Super Gecko comic book with
two fingers, like it might break.

"I was thinking it would be cool to look into Super Gecko's superpowers at Saturday Science Club next week," Stink said. "What do you think?"

"Yes!" Riley pumped her fist. "I'm also into a Korean-American superhero named Silk. Her real name is Cindy Moon. She got bitten by the same spider as Peter Parker, so she can wall-crawl like Spider-Man and Super Gecko."

"Grool!" said Stink. When Pink Hair Girl came back, he told her that he would not be selling the Super Gecko comics after all.

Goodbye, double sawbuck. Hello, Super Gecko.

Stink went back to reading the comics with his friends.

"These old ads are funny," said Webster. "Look at this one for sea monkeys!"

"*Shazam!*" said Stink. "How great would it be to have sea monkeys for pets?"

"Not so great," piped up Grandma Lou. "When I was a kid, I sent off my dollar and got some eggs in an envelope. I think they were really some kind of shrimp. All I know is they stunk to high heaven."

"Sea monkey stink bombs!" said Stink. "P.U."

"You think that's bad?" said Dad. "One time I blew *three* bucks when I sent away for invisible goldfish."

"What happened?" asked Stink.

"Nothing," said Dad. "When they finally came, I couldn't see them because they were invisible." Everybody cracked up.

"Guess what," said Webster, pointing to a page. "After Super Gecko saves the day in this one, he sheds his skin and eats it!"

"Just like a real gecko," said Sophie.

"I wish I could see an actual gecko do that!" said Stink.

"You could," said Sophie. "Did you know geckos live right here in Virginia?"

"No way!" said Webster.

"Brainstorm!" said Stink. "Let's go on a gecko hunt."

Webster jumped up. "Yeah! What are we waiting for?"

"We have to wait until it gets dark," said Sophie. "Geckos around here don't come out much during the day. That's why they're also called moon lizards."

"Spooky spaghetti!" said Stink. "Let's meet out front by the tree stump just before dark tonight."

"Hey, Stink. Your friend is buying my old art supplies," said Judy. "Ka-ching!"

Stink looked up. "Riley? You're still here?" He looked at her pile. "A box of dried-up paints and glue and half an eraser? And old *Nat Geo* magazines? Are you making a collage or something?"

Riley shrugged.

"Or something," said Judy. "At least Riley's not a lookie-loo."

Stink waved goodbye to Riley as she left. "Later, alligator," said Stink.

"Time for us to go, too," said Webster. "*Hasta mañana*, iguana!"

"See you soon, raccoon," called Sophie.

"Gotta go, geck-o!" said Webster and Sophie. *Jinx!*

"Don't forget about gecko hunting tonight," called Stink. "Be there at moon-lizard o'clock sharp."

By three o'clock, the yard sale was winding down. "Where is everybody?" asked Stink.

"It's over, Stink," said Judy. "All the good stuff is gone."

"But I didn't even make any money."

"That's because you had your head in those comic books all day."

Stink looked around. "But there's still good stuff left. Like . . . this sandbox shovel. And what about my toe socks? Wait! Nobody bought these old encyclopedias?"

"There's only *U*, *G*, and *H* left," said Judy. "Hey, it spells UGH!"

Stink picked up the *G* volume. "*G* is for *gecko*. I'm keeping this one."

"That'll be fifty cents," said Judy.

"Ugh," said Stink.

"Kidding!" said Judy. "You can pay me in toe socks."

While Stink waited for it to get dark, he practiced his gecko moves. He got a running start and tried to run up the wall. "I am one with the night! I am Super Gecko!"

CRASH! BOOM! BAM! POW! He fell—*splat*—on his behind.

"Mom! Dad!" yelled Judy. "Stink's climbing the walls!"

"No more Super Gecko in the house, Stink," said Mom. "You're getting dirty sneaker prints all over the walls."

"Toadstools!" said Stink.

The sun began to go down. At last it was half-dark. Twilight. Moon-lizard o'clock! "Gecko time!" called Stink.

Webster came with pocket binoculars. Sophie brought a zoomable flashlight. And Stink had his SpyXR night-vision goggles.

Stink had read up on geckos in the G encyclopedia. He showed his friends a drawing of gecko tracks. "Look for footprints like these: five toes and

round toe pads."

"Check," said Webster and Sophie.

"Or, look for this." Stink drew a line with a stick in the dirt. "That could be tail drag from a gecko."

"Where should we look?" asked Webster.

"Look in cracks where they might be hiding," said Stink. "Or near lights. Better yet, look on the walls of the house. Geckos have gazillions of teeny tiny hairs that act like glue and help them stick to walls. Report back in five."

Webster peered into sidewalk cracks.

Sophie scanned the walls of the Moody house. Stink searched around the base of the lamppost.

"In brightest day, in darkest night, no gecko shall escape my sight!" said Stink. "It's like what Green Lantern says while he's waiting for his power ring to charge."

"I found prints in the mud!" said Webster. Stink came running. But it was only paw prints from Mouse the cat.

"I found tail drag!" called Sophie. Stink came running again.

"That's where I drew with a stick," said Stink.

"Oopsie," said Sophie.

They searched a while longer, but all they found was a bottle cap, an acorn hat, and a piece of sidewalk chalk. No sign of geckos.

"This is *loco*," said Webster. "Gecko tracks are tiny. How are we ever going to find them in the dark?"

Sophie aimed her flashlight on a pile of leaves and zoomed in. "Geckos like to hide in leaf litter."

"Geckos can make themselves look like leaves," said Stink.

"So how will we know if they're hiding in there?" Webster asked.

"Listen for chirps," said Stink. "Geckos are the gabbiest of all lizards. They make all kinds of chirps, like this: click-click, squeak-squeak, cheep-chack-chirp."

"Shh," said Webster. "I think I hear something."

They got as quiet as a gecko shedding its skin.

"Are you sure that wasn't just Stink doing his gecko imitation?" Sophie asked.

"No, listen." *Crick-et, crick-et. Rib-bet. Rib-bet.*

"That's a cricket," said Sophie,

sweeping the yard with the beam of her flashlight.

"Or a frog," said Stink. He leaned in closer to listen. As he did, something caught his eye. Something gleaming in the beam of Sophie's flashlight.

"Hey, Sophie, zoom in on that," he said, pointing.

Sophie aimed her light on the side-walk. They moved in and found a trail of glittering, sticky drops, like tiny footprints. They followed the sticky footprint trail down the sidewalk, across the grass, and over to a tree stump.

Curiouser and curiouser.

Sophie shined the light down into the hollow of the tree stump. Stink pulled out a shiny red . . . candy wrapper.

"Drat. It's just trash," said Stink. "From a candy bar."

"But wait. There's something else in here, too." Sophie pointed to a folded-up piece of notebook paper. "What's that?"

Stink could not believe his night-vision-goggle eyes! He opened the wad of paper. "This one's not trash. It's a note!"

"Ooh, maybe it's a secret message from fairies!" said Sophie of the Elves.

"Or some kind of greeting from aliens!" said Webster. "Read it!"

The note was not in printing. The note was not in cursive. The note was made up of letters cut out from magazines. "Hey. There's a chocolate thumbprint in the corner. Maybe it's from the Candy Bar Bandit."

"What's it say? What's it say?" asked Webster and Sophie.

Stink's eyes got big. Stink's eyes got as round as gecko eyes. "I can't believe it. A note to me from Super Gecko."

Wait just a cheep-chack-chirp minute! Super Gecko was not real. Super Gecko was a comic book superhero. Super Gecko could not have written the note.

"This has to be a joke," said Stink. "Somebody's playing a trick on me." Stink squinted at his friends. "You guys wrote the note, didn't you? You wanted to fool me into thinking that Super Gecko was real and that he wrote me a letter."

"Not me," said Webster.

"Don't look at me," said Sophie.

"Pinkie swear?" asked Stink.

Webster and Sophie locked pinkie fingers.

"Repeat after me," said Stink.

"Pinkie, pinkie cowbell

Whoever tells a lie

Has to smell a sea monkey

Or get a pie in the eye."

Webster and Sophie repeated the rhyme.

"Now seal your pinkie promise with your thumbs," said Stink.

Webster and Sophie touched thumbs. That's when Stink knew that his friends were telling the truth.

But if not them, who?

GECKO FACTS

"HELP! I'm caught!"

"Oh, wait. I'll just shed my tail!"

Most geckos are nocturnal—they come out at night.

Geckos are eyeball lickers! That's how they keep their eyes clean.

SQUEAK! HISS! BARK! CHIRP!

Call me! Geckos are the gabbiest of lizards.

Staring contest! You lose! Geckos don't blink because they have no eyelids.

Will the real Super Gecko please stand up!

Batman had a secret identity—Bruce Wayne. Wonder Woman had a secret identity—Diana Prince. Spider-Man had a secret identity—Peter Parker. If only Stink could figure out the secret identity of Super Gecko the Note Sender.

Maybe it was Dad or Mom. *Light bulb!* Stink ran downstairs and leafed through Mom and Dad's magazines. But nothing had been cut out. Not a single letter.

Judy? Stink ran back upstairs. "Can I see your Me Collage?" he asked.

"Sure," said Judy. She took it down from her bulletin board. "How come?"

"Top secret," said Stink. "Back in a flash." Just like a forensic scientist studying handwriting, he looked at the letters on the note. Then he compared them to the letters on the collage.

Judy's letters were super messy. The

edges were jagged. And there were glue bumps everywhere. The letters in the gecko note were super neat. Straight edges. No glue bumps. Stink knew for a fact that Judy was no good with scissors. But this letter writer was some kind of scissors superhero and sneaky sticky-glue villain.

"Here's your Me Collage back," said Stink. "I can see why you flunked Scissors in preschool."

"Huh?"

"Any chance I could take your fingerprints?"

"Goodbye, Sherlock," said Judy, nudging him out the door.

Sherlock! As in Sherlock Holmes, Greatest Detective Ever! Sherlock Holmes knew all about footprints and secret codes and handwriting. All Stink had to do was return to the scene of the crime. And use forensic science to solve the case, just like Sherlock.

Just like Saturday Science Club!

The next morning Stink grabbed a magnifying glass and tweezers and stuff. He ran out front to the tree stump.

First he had to protect the scene of the crime. Stink unrolled a yellow streamer and wrote DO NOT CROSS on it. He wrapped it around the tree stump three times.

Next he had to collect evidence. Maybe the secret note writer had left behind a strand of hair or a piece of clothing. But Stink did not find a single hair. Not one scrap of cloth. He found a muddy cat's-eye marble, an

old Band-Aid (yuck!), and a piece of red candy-bar wrapper with a *K* on it. He carefully picked up each one with his tweezers and put them in plastic baggies.

Now it was time for Stink to use his Super Powers of Deduction.

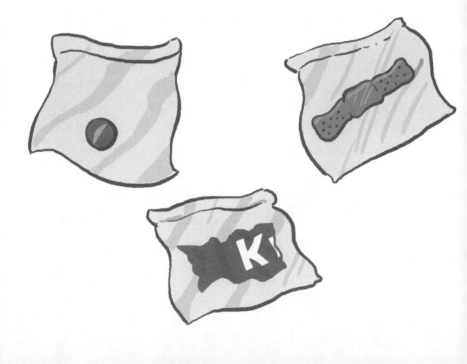

Grandma Lou liked cat's-eye marbles. She had jars of them. But this one looked like it had been outside for a long time. The note, on the other hand, hadn't even been rained on. Judy wore Band-Aids. She even collected them. But this did not look like one of her Crazy Strips. Besides, Judy didn't have any cuts or scrapes right now. And the candy wrapper? Stink tried to think of somebody who liked Kit Kat bars.

Mrs. Soso, their neighbor, waved to Stink from her yard. A witness! A real, live, actual, next-door witness. "Hi, Mrs. Soso!" called Stink. He went over

to the fence. "Have you seen anybody hanging around this tree stump?"

"Just an old raccoon," said Mrs. Soso, chuckling.

"Anybody human? Like somebody who was writing a note. Or wearing a Band-Aid. Or eating a candy bar."

"Hmm. Let's see. A mysterious note-writing, Band-Aid–wearing, candy-bar-eating bandit. Nope. Not lately."

"Thanks anyway!" said Stink.

So much for witnesses. This was a job for Saturday Science Club forensic science! Stink took out his magnifying glass. He examined the sticky footprints leading to the tree stump. He used his Super Powers of Observation.

A.) The suspect owned a bottle of clear glue or rubber cement. *Judy? Judy was always doing arts and crafts stuff. But Stink had already ruled her out.*

B.) The suspect knew that geckos were super sticky. *Webster? Sophie? Ack! It could be anybody. Everybody knew geckos had super sticking power.*

C.) The suspect was neat and tidy. *The drops were not spilled. They were placed in a straight line an inch apart. Definitely NOT Judy. ?????*

Stink scribbled everything down in a notebook. But even with his Super Powers of Observation he couldn't figure it out. So he tore out a page and wrote a note. *WHO ARE YOU?* He left the note in the tree stump.

Stakeout time. Stink watched the tree stump until he went to school. Stink watched the tree stump when he got home from school. Stink watched the tree stump until bedtime. Despite his sharp-eyed stakeout of the stump, he did not see one single candy-bar-eating Band-Aid Bandit.

What he *did* see was that his note was gone! But the bandit was as invisible as Black Panther when he wore his special suit.

Every day, Stink looked for an answer to his note. He looked for one after karate. He looked for one after dinner.

He looked for one before bedtime.

By Wednesday, Stink had just about given up. Even if there was a new note, it could have been stolen by a midnight raccoon. Or been eaten by a chipmunk!

He was just about to go inside to bed when he saw something in the beam of his flashlight.

A folded piece of notebook paper. It had to be a note!

But Stink could not read the note. If it was a note, the writing was invisible!

This trickster sure was getting trickier. Who would leave him a blank note?

Or . . . maybe . . . it was invisible ink!

Stink ran inside and held the paper under a light. At first all he could see was a chocolate fingerprint. The Candy Bar Bandit was back!

Then Stink noticed the ghosts of letters pressed into the paper. Wait just a Kit Kat minute!

Stink ran and got a pencil. He rubbed the pencil across the paper and—*presto!*—letters appeared.

I AM MAKING A COMEBACK. AN ALL-NEW
SUPER GECKO IS IN YOUR FUTURE. DON'T BELIEVE IT?
GO TO DOCTOR OCTOPUS, THE COMIC BOOK STORE.
SEEING IS BELIEVING.
SIGNED, SUPER GECKO

A comeback! Could this mean . . . an all-new Super Gecko comic book?

He ran inside to call Grandma Lou. He told her about the Candy Bar Bandit. He told her about the hidden message. He told her about the possibility of a brand-new Super Gecko comic book. "We have to get to Doctor Octopus!"

Stink told her. "We have to find out if it's true."

"I'd love to take you to the comic book store," said Grandma Lou.

"They're open till eight on Thursdays," said Stink.

"It's a date," said Grandma Lou. "See you tomorrow, Super Stink!"

See page 150 for answers!

*oot-Toot!*

"Grandma Lou's here!" Stink called to Judy, who insisted on tagging along.

Stink and Judy piled into the back of Grandma Lou's Mini Cooper. When they got to Doctor Octopus and parked, Stink flew like the Flash down the stairs to the underground comic book store.

Whoosh! When he opened the front door, it made a funny sound. *Shhh-wee. Shhh-wee.*

"Hey, it sounds like the doors on star-ship *Enterprise* in *Star Trek!*"

"Rare!" said Judy.

"It looks like a dungeon down here," said Grandma Lou.

Bins and spinner racks were full of floppy comic books. The shop was wallpapered with superhero posters, even on the ceiling. *Bam! Boing! Wow! Pow-Pow!* Action figures and Hulk hands and Black Panther claws lined the counter. Behind the counter was

a comic book signed by Spider-Man himself!

A girl with pink hair stood behind the counter. "Hey, I know you!" Stink said.

"I came to your yard sale," said the girl. "Did you change your mind about selling your Super Gecko comics?"

"Nope," said Stink, turning red. "Sorry about that."

"Then you must be here about the new Super Gecko." Pink Hair Girl pointed to a sign hanging up behind her that said *HELLO, FUN!*

"Hello, fun? That's what Super Gecko says! Wait. Hold everything. So it's true? There's going to be a brand-new comic book about Super Gecko?"

The girl nodded. Stink blurted the big news to Judy and Grandma Lou. He showed them a cardboard standee of the new Super Gecko. It was taller than Stink. The new Super Gecko was leaner and greener, with pop-out eyes and scaly skin.

"Look at all this stuff!" Stink said. There were Super Gecko hats, Super

Gecko pj's, Super Gecko temporary tattoos, Super Gecko bumper stickers, Super Gecko key chains, Super Gecko 2-in-1 pencil-pens.

Pink Hair Girl said, "We're getting ready for Saturday."

"Saturday?" asked Stink.

"The first comic book of the brand-new Super Gecko series comes out this Saturday. *Super Gecko vs. Lizardo, Volume Zero.*"

Yeet! Stink could hardly wait two more days. "How much?" he asked.

"Three ninety-nine. Come early because we're going to sell out fast."

Drat! Stink was pretty sure he only had three dollars in his piggy bank.

"Wanna know a secret?" Pink Hair Girl asked. Stink nodded. "I got to read a sneak preview."

"What? Tell me! What's it about?" said Stink.

"I'll just tell you this," said Pink Hair Girl. "The new Super Gecko puts an *o* on the end of everything. Like he says *Cool-o* and *Smart-o*."

"Neat-o!" said Stink. Pink Hair Girl went to help a customer.

"I want to get something Super Gecko," Stink told Grandma Lou. "But I think I should save my three dollars to try to buy *Super Gecko vs. Lizardo, Volume Zero*, the new comic book, on Saturday."

"Tell you what," said Grandma Lou. "You and Judy can each pick out one thing to take home today. My treat."

Judy picked up the Super Gecko Supersonic Grip 2-in-1 pencil-pen right away.

Stink picked up the Super Gecko trading cards. He put them down. Stink picked up the Super Gecko tattoos. He put them down. Stink picked up the Super Gecko finger pads. He put them down.

"Stink, you're taking forever. Grandma Lou, while Stink is busy not making up his mind, I'm going to go look at Squirrel Girl stuff."

Stink kept looking. Stink kept not deciding. He could hear Judy whispering to somebody in the Squirrel Girl section. Was she talking to herself? Or whispering to Grandma Lou?

"Hey, Stink! Look who I found," said Judy, leading somebody over by the arm.

Riley Rottenberger!

"Whoa!" said Stink. "What a co-inky-dink! What are you doing here?"

Riley grinned. "Remember how I told you about my favorite superhero, Silk?"

"The girl who got bitten by the same radioactive spider that got Spider-Man?"

"Yes! When you buy a Silk comic book, you can put your name in a jar for a prize," said Riley. "So I did it last week. And guess what? My name got picked and I came to get my prize. Look!"

Riley reached into her pocket and pulled out a coin. Stamped on it was an *S* that looked like a lightning bolt, with a spiderweb behind it.

Stink read the coin. "*Second Bitten*. Grool!"

"And this." Riley lifted up her sleeve to show off her rub-on spiderweb tattoo.

"Neat-o!" said Stink. He turned back to Grandma Lou. "I think I'll get the gecko tattoos. They glow in the dark."

"Finally!" said Judy.

When they were all checked out, Stink called to Riley. "See you at Saturday Science Club!"

"Not if I see you first," said Riley. "At school tomorrow!"

As they climbed into the car, Stink asked Judy, "What were you guys whispering about?"

After a pause, Judy said, "About this. Here." She gave Stink her Super Gecko 2-in-1 pencil-pen. "You can have it, for keeps. I know how much you like Super Gecko."

"What a nice thing to do for your brother, Judy," said Grandma Lou.

"Hello, fun!" said Stink. "Now I can draw my own comics with this way-official Super Gecko pencil-pen! Thanks-o!"

COMIC BOOK FUN FACTS

The Library of Congress has the world's largest collection of comic books. 140,000 issues!

And the award for Most Valuable Comic Book goes to: Action Comics #1 (1938), where Superman first appeared. Price: $4,620,000!

The first Saturday in May is FREE COMIC BOOK DAY.

FREE?

YUP!

Civil rights icon John Lewis learned about Martin Luther King Jr. from, you guessed it, a comic book!

Famous people who read comic books:

BARACK OBAMA
RACHEL MADDOW
EMINEM
STEPHEN KING
MARK HAMILL
(aka LUKE SKYWALKER)

Ever heard of Obadiah Oldbuck? He starred in the first US comic book in 1842.

Oldbuck looks like an odd duck!

Ninety-nine cents.

Ninety-nine pennies. Nine dimes plus nine pennies. Nineteen nickels plus four pennies. Three quarters plus twenty-four pennies. One dollar minus one penny.

No matter which way he looked at it, Stink came up short. He only had three dollars. How was he going to come up with ninety-nine cents by Saturday?

It was already Friday. Stink felt a supersonic scream coming on.

In morning Math, they were counting money. Fake coins. Plastic pennies, dimes, and quarters. Stink was the fastest money counter in Class 2D. Too bad it wasn't real money. As in ninety-nine cents' worth.

At lunch, Stink searched the cafeteria floor for any not-plastic coins that somebody might have dropped. At recess, he crawled around on the playground, looking for lost pennies.

"What are you doing?" asked Webster.

"Looking for pennies that somebody might have dropped. I need to come up with ninety-nine cents by tomorrow to buy *Super Gecko vs. Lizardo, Volume Zero.*"

"C'mon, Stink," called Sophie. "We're playing freeze tag. You have to unfreeze me."

"Wait. I think I see a nickel." Stink picked up something silver and shiny. "Rats. It's just a pop top." He tossed it into the recycle bin. "Hey, Webster, don't you always carry a nickel in your pocket?"

"No way am I giving up my lucky Buffalo nickel," said Webster.

"How about you, Sophie? You always have a state quarter for emergency gum, right?"

"I, um, I already had a gum emergency today," sputtered Sophie. "Sorry."

"Some friends," muttered Stink.

As soon as Stink got home from school, he went straight to the couch. He stuck his hand behind the cushions and felt around. Nothing. He stuck his hand in a little deeper. And a little deeper.

Ka-ching! A penny, a nickel, and a button.

Upstairs, Stink checked the pockets of all his pants. Stink checked in the dust bunnies under his bed. He even checked under his pillow—just in case he had missed something from the Tooth Fairy.

He searched for half an hour, but all

he came up with was a lousy six cents.

"What's wrong?" Judy asked, coming into his room.

"I need money," said Stink. "Will you buy this button for ninety-three cents?"

"Even if I wanted to buy a button," said Judy, "I don't have any money."

"What about your yard sale money?"

"I blew it on a Squirrel Girl comic at Doctor Octopus," said Judy.

Stink started to hiccup. Not the hiccups! Stink always got the hiccups when he was stressed out.

"C'mon, Stink, maybe we can think of somewhere else to look," said Judy. "Like the couch. Or under your bed. Or under your pillow."

"Did it, done, and done," said Stink.

"What about origami? Do you still have any dollar-bill origami frogs?"

"Good idea!" Stink dumped out his origami, which he found *after* the yard sale. There were origami sharks and ninja stars and jumping frogs. But they were all made from plain old paper. No dollar bills.

"How about that magic set you got from Grandma Lou? Didn't it have a disappearing coin trick?"

Stink ran to his closet and pulled out the magic set. He looked through all the magic tricks. "Drat. No coin. I guess I made it disappear!" said Stink.

"Dump out your piggy bank, and we'll count again," said Judy. "Just in case."

Stink shook his piggy bank. He shook it some more. Out fell a folded piece of not-origami paper. "Hey, what's this?"

Judy shrugged. "I'm going to say it looks like a note. Open it."

Stink unfolded the paper. It *was* a note! A not-invisible-ink note! It had cut-out letters just like the first note he'd found in the tree stump.

"What does it say?" Judy asked.

Stink read the note.

LOOK in THE TREE STUMP
SIGNED, SUPER
GECKO

Stink couldn't help himself. He ran down the stairs and out the front door and over to the tree stump. Judy ran after him.

Stink reached inside and felt around.

A plastic baggie. Not a plastic baggie of evidence. A plastic baggie of money. Moola! Cashola! It was mostly pennies, but there was an old nickel, a couple of silver coins, and at least one shiny quarter.

"There must be over a hundred cents in here!" said Stink.

"I bet there's like one hundred twenty-seven cents in there," said Judy.

Stink narrowed his eyes, peering at Judy. "It's you, isn't it?" said Stink. "You put the note in my piggy bank. You're Super Gecko."

"I wish," said Judy. "But you know me. I never have any money." She pointed to the note. "And I could never cut out letters that neat. Remember? I flunked Scissors."

"I still think it's you."

"It's not me, Stink. I'm just a red herring."

"What's a red herring?"

"It's like a fake clue. A clue that makes it look like it's me, but it's not me."

"Who else could put a note in my piggy bank? Nobody's been in my room but you."

"This sneaky Super Gecko must be invisible," said Judy.

"Oh, yeah! Maybe they can bend light waves! Maybe they were right here in my room beside me and I didn't even know!"

"At least the money's not invisible, am I right?" said Judy.

"Right," said Stink, shaking the coins

in the bag. "With my three dollars, and the money I found in the couch, this is more than enough. Wa-hoo!" He pumped a fist in the air. "*Super Gecko vs. Lizardo, Volume Zero*, you are mine!"

Saturday! Hello, fun!

Stink stood at the sink, holding a wet paper towel on his arm for twenty seconds. *Prest-o!*

"Check out my Super Gecko tattoo!" said Stink. "This is going to be the best-ever Saturday times infinity."

"Why's that?" asked Mom.

"*First* because it's superhero science day at Saturday Science Club," said Stink. "And *second* because the first Super Gecko reboot comic book is coming out today!"

"I admit I can't wait to see it," said Dad.

"Well, you won't have to wait long," said Stink. But . . . wait just a spooky-spaghetti second! "Oh, no!" moaned Stink, sinking to the floor. "This is not the best-ever Saturday. It's the worst times infinity!"

"Wha—?" Judy started.

"It just hit me. Saturday Science

Club starts at ten o'clock and the comic book store opens at the exact same time. Goodbye, fun."

"What a sticky-wicky situation!" Dad teased.

"Doctor Octopus will be open all day," said Judy. "Just go *after* science club."

"But what if they run out of the new Super Gecko comic by the time I get there? No way do I want to miss superhero science, but I can't be in two places at once."

"Not unless you can turn into a time-traveling superhero by ten a.m.," said Judy.

"Drats-o!" said Stink.

"No worries," said Mom. "Riley's mom just called and said they'll be making a beeline for Doctor Octopus as soon as Science Club is over. Riley thought you might want to go with them, too."

ZOOM! Did he ever!

"Riley Rottenberger must have the mind-reading powers of Superman," said Stink. *Spooky spaghetti!*

✳ ✳ ✳

Superhero science was the best. As it turned out, almost all superhero powers were based on real science! Who knew? They tried on night-vision goggles to learn how Batman might see in the dark. They got to make their own lightning bolts like the Flash, using balloons to create static elec-tricity. And they learned how Super Gecko could climb walls with incred-ible sticking power due to van der Waals forces.

Superman could soar over Met-ropolis thanks to Newton's Second Law of Motion. Silk would have to eat 750 eggs for enough protein to shoot spider-webs from her fingers, but still . . .

Stink and Riley made superhero slime and stretched it halfway across the room to test how far Elastigirl might be able to stretch. They had water-drop races where they blew

through a straw to see who could get their water droplet across a piece of wax paper the fastest. After the race, Mrs. Rottenberger explained all about surface tension and how the Flash could walk on water.

As soon as Saturday Science Club was over, Stink and Riley ran to the Rottenbergers' car.

"Science is the best," said Stink. "Too bad we can't use Newton's Second Law of Motion to zoom through the air to the comic book store."

"I don't think Newton knew about traffic laws," said Mrs. Rottenberger.

"We need a superpower that changes all the red lights to green," Riley said.

When they pulled into the parking lot, Stink gasped. "Great Casper's ghost! Look at all these Geckoheads."

"The line is all the way out the door," said Riley.

Yeet! Stink's stomach dropped. "I hope they don't run out!" said Stink. "Too bad we don't have hundreds of teeny-tiny gecko hairs on our feet that stick like glue. We could leap this tall building in a single bound and sneak in through the back."

"Gecko power!" yelled Riley.

"I bet Super Gecko could scale these walls in five seconds flat, right, Mrs. Rottenberger? Or you might say he could scale these *van der Waals* in no time. Get it? It's a science joke."

Riley and her mom laughed. "I get it," said Riley. "Because van der Waals is that force that makes geckos

stick to the wall. Right, Mom?"

"That's right," said Mrs. Rotten-berger. "I don't think you two have ever paid this much attention in Saturday Science Club before. Maybe we should do superhero science again next week."

"Hello, fun!" said Stink.

CHALLENGE A FRIEND TO A WATER-DROP RACE!

1 TAKE A SHEET OF WAX PAPER AND DRAW A STARTING LINE AND A FINISH LINE.

2 DRIP TWO DROPS OF WATER ONTO THE WAX PAPER AT THE STARTING LINE. READY, SET, RACE!

3 BLOW THROUGH A STRAW TO MOVE A WATER DROP ACROSS THE WAX PAPER.

4 THE PLAYER WHOSE WATER DROP REACHES THE FINISH LINE FIRST WINS!

SCIENCE HINT: WAX PAPER DOES NOT ABSORB WATER. THE SURFACE TENSION OF THE WATER MAKES A BLOB. THE BLOB STICKS TO ITSELF INSTEAD OF TO THE WAX ON THE PAPER.

As soon as they parked at Doctor Octopus, Stink shot out of the car faster than a speeding bullet.

"Hip, hip, hip, and away you go!" shouted Riley, waiting for her mom. "I'll catch up with you inside."

"Stink! Over here!" It was Judy, with Webster and Sophie of the Elves.

"Wowzer! What are you guys doing here?" Stink asked.

Judy held up Stink's baggie of coins. "You forgot your money. So Mom and Dad dropped us off and went to get coffee next door."

Judy handed the money to Stink.

"Thanks!" said Stink. They were almost to the front of the line. "Does it look like they have enough?"

"I can't tell," said Sophie.

Stink crossed his fingers. "As soon as I get mine, I'm going to read it at the speed of lightning like the Flash. He can read a whole library in seconds."

"Stink, you're up!" said Judy.

Stink rushed up to the counter. He handed the baggie full of coins to Pink Hair Girl. "I have enough in here for the comic plus tax," said Stink.

"There's no tax," said Pink Hair Girl.

"Funny story," said Stink. "How I got the money, I mean. See, I only had three dollars—"

"Stink, you're holding up the line," said Judy.

"Let's step to the side while I count your money," said Pink Hair Girl. A guy took over while she dumped out Stink's coins on the counter and began to count, starting with the pennies. "Two, four, six, eight . . . Hey, one of these is a Buffalo nickel. Are you sure you want to use this? And this one is the California state quarter. I hardly ever see these."

Wha? "What are those doing in there?" Stink looked around for Webster and Sophie, but they'd stepped out of the line and disappeared into the crowd.

"Let's see if you have enough with-out them," said Pink Hair Girl. "Ten, twelve, fourteen, sixteen . . . Wait. What's this?" She handed it to Stink.

This one was a shiny silver coin with a spiderweb on it. *And* it had an *S* that looked like a lightning bolt. *And* it said *SECOND BITTEN.*

Poof! Whap! Snap! Zak!

All of a sudden, speedier than Super Gecko could scale a building, Stink knew who had made the sticky-wicky gecko footprints. Stink knew who had sent the secret notes. Stink knew, once and for all, who had put the money in the tree stump. His spidey senses were tingling all over!

Will the real Super Gecko please stand up!

"Here's your comic book," said Pink Hair Girl, "and your change."

Stink grabbed his comic book and his change. He held the three coins in his hand and went to find Judy and his friends, including the Candy Bar Bandit.

"It was you!" he cried. "You're the secret Super Gecko. It was you all along, Riley Rottenberger!"

Riley hid behind her braids. When she pulled her braids away from her face, she was smiling ear to ear. "Okay, I give! It was me!"

"I knew it!" said Stink, jumping up and down.

"First it just started with me leaving the note. I cut letters out of magazines I bought at your yard sale and glued them to notebook paper so you wouldn't know my handwriting. Later, I got Sophie and Webster to help me come up with the ninety-nine cents you needed to buy the new comic book."

"But how did you ever get that note into my piggy bank?"

"Yours truly," said Judy, raising her

hand. "Remember when we ran into Riley here the other day? That's when she gave me the note and I snuck it into your piggy bank."

"See? This is why I need a password-protected piggy bank!" said Stink. He handed back the coins. "Webster, I can't believe you were going to give up your Buffalo nickel. Sophie, you gave

up your emergency gum money for me. And Riley, this is your special Silk coin."

"Even though it's not real money, I

thought maybe Doctor Octopus would let you use it or something if you didn't have enough."

"I don't know how to thank you guys," said Stink.

"You can start by sharing your comic book," said Webster.

"I promise," said Stink, "as soon as I read it ten times, you'll be the first ones to read it." Webster and Sophie made frowny faces.

"Hardee-har-har!" said Stink. "Just kidding!"

"Oops," said Riley. "My mom's been waiting in line for me. Be right back."

Stink and Webster and Sophie plopped on the floor and hunched over the comic book. Stink closed his eyes and breathed in the smell of new ink. He could hardly believe he was holding *Super Gecko vs. Lizardo, Volume Zero.*

"Super Gecko is going to destroy Lizardo. I just know it!" said Stink.

When Riley rejoined them, Stink was reading the comic book aloud. "Lizardo's hot on your tail, Gecko. Let's *squamata* outta here!"

"Hold on. Don't tell me what happens. I have to catch up," said Riley.

When it was time to go, Mom and Dad had to practically drag Stink out of the store.

"Okay. Let's *squamata* outta here," said Stink. "Oh, wait! There's one thing I have to do before we go. I need to get Super Gecko to sign my comic book."

"He's here?" asked Webster, looking around.

"He's here?" asked Sophie, looking around.

"How can he be here?" asked Riley. "You know he's not real, right?"

"*She's* right here," said Stink. He handed the comic book to Riley. Then he handed her his Super Gecko Super-Grip 2-in-1 pencil-pen. "Your autograph, please."

Riley Rottenberger clicked the Super Grip from pencil to pen. She opened the comic book to the first page and wrote:

Cool-o! Neat-o! Spooky spaghetti-o!

Megan McDonald

is the author of the popular Judy Moody and Stink series. She says, "Once, while I was visiting a class, the kids chanted, 'Stink! Stink! Stink!' as I entered the room. In that moment, I knew that Stink had to have a series all his own." Megan McDonald lives in California.

Peter H. Reynolds

is the illustrator of all the Judy Moody and Stink books. He says, "Stink reminds me of myself growing up: dealing with a sister prone to teasing and bossing around—and having to get creative in order to stand tall beside her." Peter H. Reynolds lives in Massachusetts.

BE SURE TO CHECK OUT ALL OF STINK'S ADVENTURES!

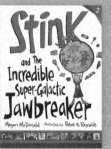

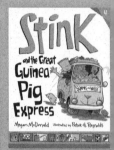

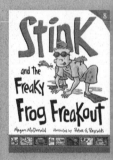

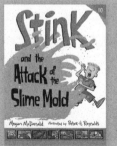